Nursery Rhymes

Hey, Diddle, Diddle

and Other Best-loved Rhymes

alphabet
soup™

an imprint of

WINDMILL
BOOKS™

New York

Published in 2009 by Windmill Books, LLC
303 Park Avenue South, Suite # 1280, New York, NY 10010-3657

Illustrations by Ulkutay & Co. Ltd.
Editor: Rebecca Gerlings
Compiler: Paige Weber

　　　　Publisher Cataloging Data

Hey, diddle, diddle and other best-loved rhymes / edited by Rebecca Gerlings.
p.　　　cm. – (Nursery rhymes)
Contents: Hey, diddle, diddle—Old King Cole—Pussy-cat, pussy-cat—
It's raining, it's pouring—Hush, little baby—Ding, dong, bell—
One, two, buckle my shoe—Pat-a-cake—Jack Sprat—Star light, star bright.
ISBN 978-1-60754-125-7 (library binding)
ISBN 978-1-60754-126-4 (paperback)
ISBN 978-1-60754-127-1 (6-pack)
1. Nursery rhymes　2. Children's poetry　[1. Nursery rhymes]
I. Gerlings, Rebecca　II. Mother Goose　III. Series
　　　　　　398.8—dc22

Printed in the United States

CONTENTS

Hey, Diddle, Diddle

Hey, diddle, diddle,
The cat and the fiddle,
The cow jumped over the moon.

4

The little dog laughed,
To see such a sport,
And the dish ran away with the spoon.

Old King Cole

Old King Cole was a merry old soul,
And a merry old soul was he.
He called for his pipe, and he called for his bowl,
And he called for his fiddlers three.
Every fiddler, he had a fine fiddle,

And a very fine fiddle had he.
Twee-tweedle-dee, tweedle-dee, went the fiddlers,
Tweedle-dum-dee, dum-dee-deedle-dee!
Oh, there's none so rare as can compare,
With King Cole and his fiddlers three!

Pussy-Cat, Pussy-Cat

Pussy-cat, pussy-cat,
Where have you been?
I've been to London,
To visit the Queen.

Pussy-cat, pussy-cat,
What did you there?
I frightened a little mouse
Under her chair.

9

It's Raining, It's Pouring

It's raining, it's pouring,
The old man is snoring.
He went to bed,
And bumped his head,
And couldn't get up in the morning.

Hush, Little Baby

Hush, little baby, don't say a word,
Papa's going to buy you a mockingbird.

And if that mockingbird won't sing,
Papa's going to buy you a diamond ring.

And if that diamond ring turns brass,
Papa's going to buy you a looking glass.

And if that looking glass gets broke,
Papa's going to buy you a billy goat.

And if that billy goat won't pull,
Papa's going to buy you a cart and bull.

And if that cart and bull turn over,
Papa's going to buy you a dog named Rover.

And if that dog named Rover won't bark,
Papa's going to buy you a horse and cart.

And if that horse and cart fall down,
You'll still be the sweetest little baby in town.

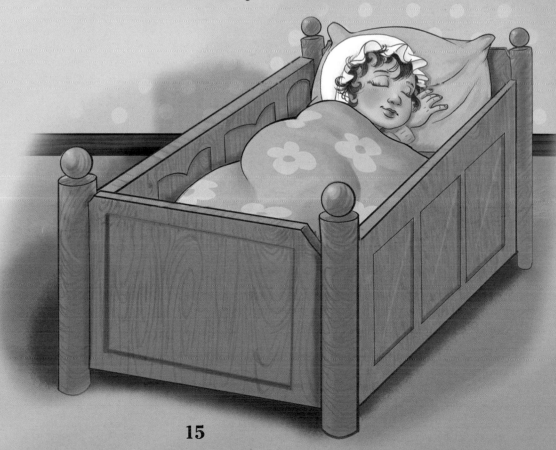

Ding, Dong, Bell

Ding, dong, bell,
Kitty's in the well!
Who put her in?
Little Tommy Lin.
Who pulled her out?
Little Johnny Stout.

What a naughty boy was that
To try to drown poor kitty-cat.
Who never did him any harm,
But killed all the mice in his father's barn!

One, Two, Buckle My Shoe

One, two,
Buckle my shoe;
Three, four,
Knock at the door;

Five, six,
Pick up sticks;
Seven, eight,
Lay them straight;

Nine, ten,
A good, fat hen;
Eleven, twelve,
Dig and delve;

Thirteen, fourteen,
Maids a-courting;
Fifteen, sixteen,
Maids in the kitchen;

Seventeen, eighteen,
Maids a-waiting;
Nineteen, twenty,
My plate's empty!

Pat-a-Cake

Pat-a-cake, pat-a-cake, baker's man,
Bake me a cake as fast as you can.
Roll it and pat it and mark it with B,
And put it in the oven for baby and me.

Jack Sprat

Jack Sprat could eat no fat,
His wife could eat no lean.
And so, between them both, you see,
They licked the platter clean.

Jack ate all the lean,
Joan ate all the fat.
The bone they picked it clean,
Then gave it to the cat.

Star Light, Star Bright

Star light, star bright,
The first star I see tonight.
I wish I may I wish I might,
Have the wish I wish tonight.

ABOUT THE RHYMES

It may come as a surprise that some nursery rhymes date back several centuries. Many people still remember these catchy rhymes in adulthood, but few know their origins. Nursery rhymes are often more than just funny poems for children. In fact, some were once very subversive!

The lyrics of nursery rhymes were sometimes used to mock the royalty and other leaders during periods when political dissidence was severely punished. It may seem strange that these issues are portrayed through children's nursery rhymes. But the result is that the rhymes form an enduring link between present and past.

Because of the way spoken history is shared between generations, nursery rhymes have many different interpretations. The following are the most popular interpretations of some of the rhymes in this book. If your favorite isn't included here, see what you can find out yourself! Each rhyme has a special story to tell.

Hey, Diddle, Diddle

This rhyme's unique appeal lies in the way it twists reality to create fanciful happenings that you would never see in real life! Have you ever seen a cow jump over the moon, or a dish run away with a spoon? Originally, "Hey, Diddle, Diddle" was called "High Diddle, Diddle," but the rhyme's name was changed in line with the evolution of the English language. Many of us remember the nonsensical, colloquial phrase "Hey Nonny No" that was often used by William Shakespeare. "Hey, Diddle, Diddle" also appeared in Shakespeare's writing. The rhyme is believed to have first been published in 1765.

Pussy-Cat, Pussy-Cat

This little feline tale can be traced back to sixteenth-century Tudor England. The cat in the story is based on the aged cat of a lady-in-waiting serving Queen Elizabeth I. One day, the cat was going about its usual wanderings around Windsor Castle when it entered the throne room and hid under the throne belonging to the queen. The naughty pet's tail touched the queen's foot, taking her by complete surprise. "Good Queen Bess" didn't hold it against the cat, instead pledging that it could explore the room at free will, in exchange for chasing out all the rodents.

Ding, Dong, Bell

This is a nursery rhyme with a moral message, due to its words becoming kinder over time. Its origins date back to the sixteenth century, during Shakespearean times, when the Elizabethan playwright used the phrase "Ding, Dong, Bell" in his stage plays, perhaps as a direction for sound effects. An earlier version of the rhyme finished with the cat's drowning. However, in the existing revised version, Little Johnny Stout comes to the cat's rescue. The rhyme has a clear message for children, teaching them not to mistreat helpless animals. It also captures the real "ding, dong" sounds a bell makes when it rings.

Pat-a-Cake

The history behind this engaging little nursery rhyme is not exactly known, but it was first published in the year 1698. It is easy for children to relate to "Pat-a-Cake" since it is based on the baking process – a popular activity for young children and their parents. The rhyme also introduces the letter "B" and links it to the word *baby*. One reason the rhyme may have stood the test of time is the fact that clapping actions can be used to accompany it.

Star Light, Star Bright

This rhyme is believed to be of late nineteenth-century American origin, and the lyrics allude to the fantasy that you can wish upon a star.

"Star Light, Star Bright" has no doubt been used on many occasions to quiet children at bedtime as they look out of the window waiting to catch their very first glimpse of starlight that evening. A very popular rhyme, its first line has been used as the title for various books and songs in more recent times.